*For Cathy Freese*

Clarion Books
a Houghton Mifflin Company imprint
215 Park Avenue South, New York, NY 10003


Printed in the USA

*Library of Congress Cataloging in Publication Data*

Galdone, Paul.
Cat goes fiddle-i-fee.
Summary: An old English rhyme names all the animals a farm boy feeds on his daily rounds.
1. Nursery rhymes, English. 2. Children's poetry, English. [1. Nursery rhymes. 2. English poetry]
I. Title.
PZ8.3.G1218Cat 1985 398'.8 85-2686
ISBN 0-89919-336-6 PA ISBN 0-89919-705-1

BVG 20 19 18 17 16 15 14 13

# Cat Goes Fiddle-i-fee

Adapted and Illustrated by
PAUL GALDONE

Clarion Books
New York

I had a cat and the cat pleased me,
I fed my cat by yonder tree.

*Cat goes fiddle-i-fee.*

I had a hen and the hen pleased me,
I fed my hen by yonder tree.

Hen goes chimmy-chuck, chimmy-chuck,
*Cat goes fiddle-i-fee.*

I had a duck and the duck pleased me,
I fed my duck by yonder tree.

Duck goes quack, quack,
Hen goes chimmy-chuck, chimmy-chuck,
*Cat goes fiddle-i-fee.*

I had a goose and the goose pleased me,
I fed my goose by yonder tree.

Goose goes swishy, swashy,
Duck goes quack, quack,
Hen goes chimmy-chuck, chimmy-chuck,
*Cat goes fiddle-i-fee.*

I had a sheep and the sheep pleased me,
I fed my sheep by yonder tree.

Sheep goes baa, baa,
Goose goes swishy, swashy,
Duck goes quack, quack,
Hen goes chimmy-chuck, chimmy-chuck,
*Cat goes fiddle-i-fee.*

I had a pig and the pig pleased me,
I fed my pig by yonder tree.

Pig goes griffy, gruffy,
Sheep goes baa, baa,
Goose goes swishy, swashy,
Duck goes quack, quack,
Hen goes chimmy-chuck, chimmy-chuck,
*Cat goes fiddle-i-fee.*

I had a cow and the cow pleased me,
I fed my cow by yonder tree.

Cow goes moo, moo,
Pig goes griffy, gruffy,
Sheep goes baa, baa,
Goose goes swishy, swashy,
Duck goes quack, quack,
Hen goes chimmy-chuck, chimmy-chuck,
*Cat goes fiddle-i-fee.*

I had a horse and the horse pleased me,
I fed my horse by yonder tree.

Horse goes neigh, neigh,
Cow goes moo, moo,
Pig goes griffy, gruffy,
Sheep goes baa, baa,
Goose goes swishy, swashy,
Duck goes quack, quack,
Hen goes chimmy-chuck, chimmy-chuck,
*Cat goes fiddle-i-fee.*

I had a dog and the dog pleased me,
I fed my dog by yonder tree.

Dog goes bow-wow, bow-wow,
Horse goes neigh, neigh,
Cow goes moo, moo,
Pig goes griffy, gruffy,
Sheep goes baa, baa,
Goose goes swishy, swashy,
Duck goes quack, quack,
Hen goes chimmy-chuck, chimmy-chuck,
*Cat goes fiddle-i-fee.*

Then Grandma came
and she fed me...

while the others dozed
by yonder tree.

*And cat went fiddle-i-fee.*